Let's build a BIG triangle!

Ready, little squares?
Climb up, up, up…

Now, we're a GIANT square!

Come on, circles – let's BOUNCE!

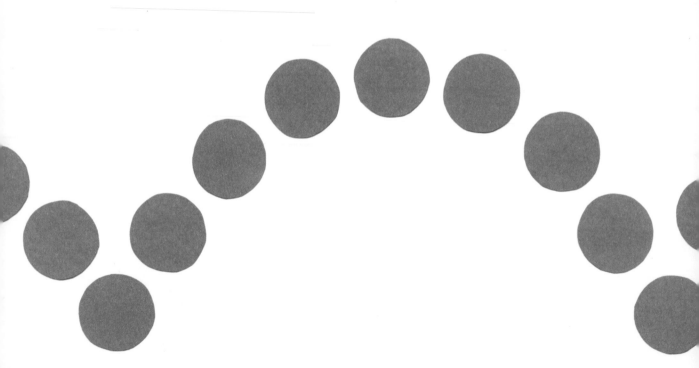

The more of us there are,
the HIGHER we will go!

Bounce! Bounce!

BUMP!

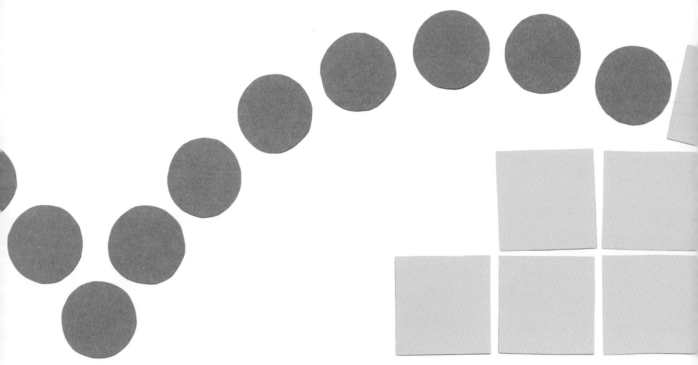

Uh-oh!
We're falling oooover!

Yes, and look
what we've made!

Hey, is everyone OK?

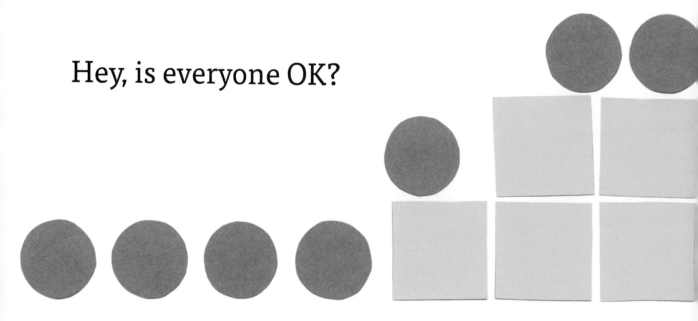

A BRAND-NEW SHAPE –
hip hip hooray!

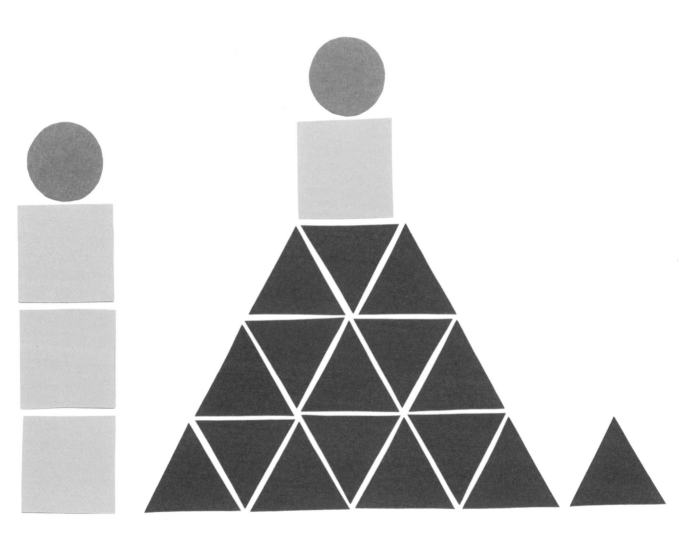

You go on top.
We'll go below...

Let's see what else
we can make!

Look! We made two houses:
one small, one tall!

Now let's build
a CASTLE.

With a tall tower ...

and a flying flag!

Ah! A lawn with a
gentle breeze ...

and two magnificent, fruity trees.

You be an apple tree,
we'll be a peach!

What about being cars?
Vroom, vroom!

Beep! Beep! You in front –
can you please hurry up?

But we're not a fast car –
we're just a little truck!

*Chugga chugga chugga chugga
CHOO CHOO!*

So let's be a train!

We've got one more idea
for something ... *FAST!*

As a supersonic rocket ship,
we can go to MARS!

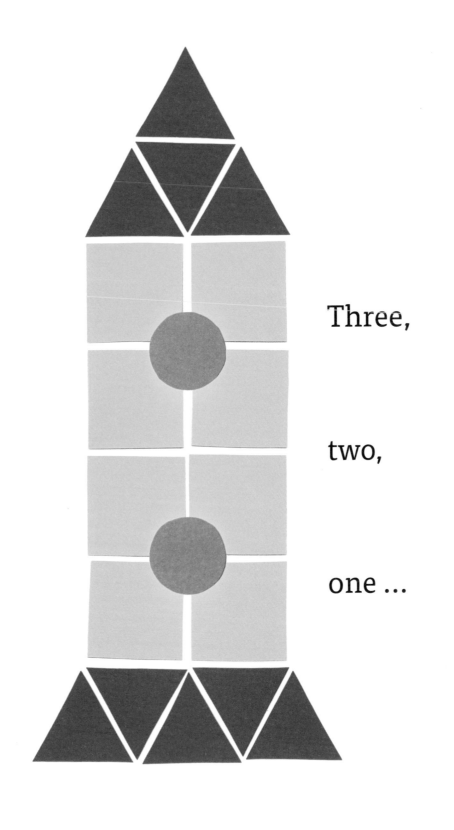

Three,

two,

one ...

BLAST OFF!

Welcome, triangles!

Welcome, squares!

Welcome, circles!

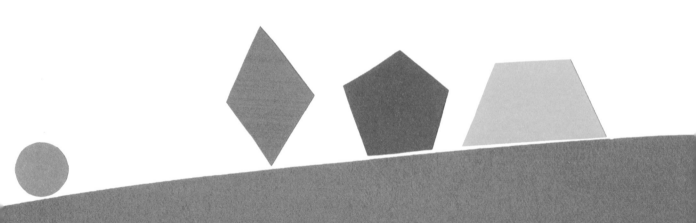